ZUBERT

CHARLIE SUTCLIFFE

THE SUN ROSE UP LIKE A PORCUPINE AS ZUBERT AND HIS MOTHER LOADED UP THE VAN...

OFF THEY WENT INTO TOWN,
DELIVERING FLOWERS TO
ALL THE BEST HOTELS.

ZUBERT WAS GETTING RATHER BORED, WAITING FOR HIS MOTHER
IN THE LOBBY OF THE SMARTEST HOTEL OF ALL, BUT HE ALWAYS CAME
PREPARED AND WAS ABOUT TO UNPACK A BOOK FROM HIS SUITCASE,

WHEN SOMETHING PECULIAR CAUGHT HIS EYE...

IT WAS A FLUTTER OF EXHAUSTED SPINGLEFRANKS SNORING!
ONE OF THE SPINGLEFRANKS SEEMED TO BE IN A TERRIBLE STATE.

'WHAT'S UP?' ASKED ZUBERT.
'WE'VE STILL GOT SO MANY ANIMALS TO HIDE BEFORE THE HOTEL
INSPECTORS ARRIVE!' STAMMERED FRANK SPINGLEFRANK.

'WHAT ANIMALS?'
WONDERED ZUBERT,
LOOKING AROUND...

'WOW!' GASPED ZUBERT.
'NOOOO!' CRIED FRANK.
'WHEEEEEE!' HOLLERED THE REST OF THE SPINGLEFRANKS, BOUNCED AWAKE BY THE BUFFALO.

'I'M NOT SLIGHTLY MAGIC LIKE YOU,' SAID ZUBERT, 'BUT CAN I HELP?' AND IN A BLINK, FRANK WAS TYING A SPARE PAIR OF WINGS ONTO ZUBERT'S BACK.

'LET'S GO GO GO!' CRIED FRANK. AND OFF THEY FLEW, UP UP UP...

ZUBERT GAVE THEM AN EXPERIMENTAL FLUTTER... AND TOOK-OFF!

TO THE ROYAL SUITE!

'OH ME!' GASPED ZUBERT.
'OH MY!' CRIED FRANK.
'OH NO!' SHOUTED THE REST OF THE SPINGLEFRANKS, 'WHAT CAN WE DO?'

ZUBERT KNEW A THING OR TWO ABOUT MONKEYS.

'BANANAS!' HE CRIED, 'MONKEYS LOVE BANANAS!'

'BANANAS!' WHOOPED THE SPINGLEFRANKS,
AND BECAUSE THEY WERE SLIGHTLY MAGIC,
BANANAS APPEARED...

AND JUST AS THE LAST MONKEY WAS TEMPTED INTO THE WARDROBE...

THE INSPECTORS MARCHED INTO THE ROOM.
THEY MUMBLED AND TUTTED AND NODDED AND NOTED. TICK TICK TICK!

'HAT WAS CLOSE', WHISPERED ZUBERT
.ET'S GO GO GO!' CRIED FRANK AND OFF THEY FLEW...

...TO THE SWIMMING POOL!

'OH ME!'
GASPED ZUBERT.
'OH MY!'
CRIED FRANK.
'OH NO!' SHOUTED
THE REST OF THE
SPINGLEFRANKS,
'WHAT CAN WE DO?'

ZUBERT KNEW
A THING OR TWO
ABOUT OCTOPUSES.
'A NET!' HE CRIED,
'WE NEED A GIANT NET!'

'GIANT NET!' WHOOPED THE SPINGLEFRANKS, AND BECAUSE THEY WERE SLIGHTLY MAGIC, A GIANT NET APPEARED...

THE INSPECTORS STRODE TOWARDS THE POOL.
THEY MUTTERED AND SHUFFLED AND
PRODDED AND POINTED.
TICK, TICK, TICK!

'OH ME!' GASPED ZUBERT.
'OH MY!' CRIED FRANK.
'OH NO!' SHOUTED THE REST OF
THE SPINGLEFRANKS, 'WHAT CAN WE DO?'

ZUBERT KNEW A THING OR TWO ABOUT ELEPHANTS.
HE KNEW THAT ELEPHANTS WERE SCARED OF MICE.
'WHAT ABOUT A MOUSE... WHO IS ALSO THE CHAMPION
OF PULLING SCARY FACES... AND IS ALSO THE FASTEST CHEF IN
THE WORLD... AND IS ALSO A GIANT SO THAT HE CAN JUGGLE BIG SAUCEPANS!'

TO THE
KITCHEN

SUGAR

POTAT

POTATO

POTAT

'A MOUSE WHO IS ALSO THE CHAMPION OF PULLING
SCARY FACES AND IS ALSO THE FASTEST CHEF IN
THE WORLD AND IS ALSO A GIANT SO THAT HE CAN
JUGGLE BIG SAUCEPANS!' THE SPINGLEFRANKS SHOUTED.

AND BECAUSE THEY WERE SLIGHTLY MAGIC,
A MOUSE APPEARED...

SIZZLE
SIZZLE

THE INSPECTORS SAT DOWN TO EAT.
THEY GOBBLED AND GUZZLED AND SNAFFLED AND SMILED.

TICK, TICK, TICK!

'WE DID IT!' GASPED ZUBERT,
AS FRANK AND THE REST OF THE SPINGLEFRANKS
BREATHED A SLIGHTLY MAGIC SIGH OF RELIEF.

CLANG!
CLANG!

THE HOTEL WAS
PICK AND SPAN
AND SO THEY
CELEBRATED WITH
SPONGE CAKE
AND POP.

'SORRY I TOOK SO LONG,'
SOOTHED ZUBERT'S MOTHER, GIVING HIM A HUG,
'WERE YOU TERRIBLY BORED WHILE I WAS GONE?'

ZUBERT SMILED, 'ONLY SLIGHTLY...'